# THE SANDMEYER REACTION

**A SHORT STORY**

BY MICHAEL CHABON

A $6 STORY

Printed in the United States of America
Book design by Laura Catherine Brown
Series editor: Samantha Schoech
ISBN 978-0-9984499-0-6

Originally published in the New York Times.

California Bookstore Day Publishing
A division of Independent Bookstore Day and
The Northern California Independent Booksellers Association

www.indiebookstoreday.com

# Author's Introduction

This is not—surprisingly—an excerpt from my novel *Moonglow*. That's surprising to me, at any rate, because the incidents related in "The Sandmeyer Reaction" were central to my idea of the novel and its protagonist almost from the start.

I had been working on the book for only a week, and was still busy introducing myself to "my grandfather"—my first-person narrator's unnamed grandfather, that is—when the book's half-dozen major plot arcs appeared all together in my imagination, sudden as a rainbow. I jotted down some notes, working quickly before the vivid images could fade: Coconut Creek—after grandmother dead—meets widow—her cat (dog?) is eaten by a python—he hunts it down—comes back to life and He is an engineer—space flight—impossible dream—prison—plastics factory—model rockets make him rich.

Then there was this:

Spy Hunt (OSS?)—Philly—an education in risk—romantic —violent.

I would tell the story, I thought, of how "my grandfather's" rough-and-tumble coming-of-age, at the fringes of South

Philadelphia's Jewish underworld, played a key role in his baptism of fire as an OSS spy during World War II. In terms of incident, it was the vaguest of all the plot arcs I envisioned, but paradoxically a sharper insight into my protagonist's personality seemed to coalesce around it. I saw that it would give me the opportunity—by what means I still didn't know—to show how in "my grandfather," an acute problem-solving intelligence was yoked to a violent and sensitive nature, in the service of a quixotic, even romantic dream.

Though it would take close to two years of writing for me to get to "The Sandmeyer Reaction," anticipating it, knowing I was headed its way, shaped my understanding of everything that led up to it. The story determined all of my narrative choices as I worked toward it, along plot zigzags of war and courtship and prison and python hunting and family madness.

For the first time in my writing life, I wasn't proceeding in straight chronological fashion from beginning to end. Instead I was following, or attempting to follow, the opioid-induced wanderings of a dying man's memory into the darkest corners of his life, as filtered through the memory of his loving grandson a quarter-century after the old man's death. As I hung in there with the narrative's swerves across time, from the late 1950s to the late 1930s to the late 1980s, from New York City to Philadelphia to Coconut Creek, Fla., the as-yet unrealized but undimmed vision of "The Sandmeyer Reaction" was my pole star. Working steadily toward it, I never lost my way.

When, at last, I arrived at what felt like the proper time to begin to tell the story, I began with deep and careful research. I amassed and devoured materials, paper and electronic, related to

Jewish South Philly, the heyday of pool hustling, racetrack life, the history of jukeboxes, the OSS's real-life "Q Branch" and its remarkable director, Stanley Lovell. Lovell's career had first become known to me through his wonderful memoir, "Of Spies and Stratagems," beloved by my nonfictional, scare-quoteless grandfather, whose old Pocket Books edition I now reread.

Feeling fully provisioned with raw facts sufficient to the telling of various gilt- and ironclad lies, ready to take a crack at the thing, I went off to the MacDowell Colony, in Peterborough, N.H. I devoted the whole of a precious two-week residency to writing the first of several drafts. Those two weeks were equaled in their hallucinatory intensity, at that point, only by the five-day period I had spent writing the Antarctic "Radioman" section of *The Amazing Adventures of Kavalier & Clay* years before. It was a thrilling plunge into a past I had, by that point, nearly come to consider my own. Though I knew that the episode was going to need heavy revision, I felt certain that, once revised, "The Sandmeyer Reaction" would be what I had always wanted it to be, and do what I had needed it to do.

Two years after that—this past March—I completed a final revision of *Moonglow*. That month unfurled as yet another, intensely focused, trancelike spell of days in the novel's history, a history unlike that of any other book I've written. In that month I wrote, rewrote, revised and polished 80 new pages, pages I could never have written, could not have known to write, before then. Scant weeks before the book was due back to my publisher, I came to understand 90 percent of everything that turned out to be most important about "my grandfather," "my grandmother," their marriage and the world they live in.

At the end of March, when I got to the end of the novel one last time, I sat down to read the manuscript. Not quite "reading" it, exactly; stalking it, slithering along it, hunting in its sawgrass for stylistic infelicities, typos, boring sentences, clichés and gags that, face it, Chabon, just never were going to work. Everything seemed to be about as OK as I was ever going to get it, or at least that's what I thought—right up till I got to "The Sandmeyer Reaction." I was not more than four or five pages into the episode—knowing, by heart, everything that was about to befall "my grandfather" in the pages to follow—when I felt a cold clutch in my abdomen, the balling of some icy interior fist. It was a fist I know well: The Fist of Dread, and its cold clenching can only ever be translated, I have managed after many years to learn, by a monosyllable: Wrong.

I ignored the feeling—this was the pole star, the anchor, the heart of the book!—and kept reading. But the further I read into the episode, the tighter the grip of dread became on my gut. Wrong. Wrong, Chabon. Stop. Something is wrong here.

In its detail, in its rhythm, in its presentation of characters in conflict with their anger, their memories, their broken affections for each other, everything seemed all right with "The Sandmeyer Reaction." (If that were not true, this passage would have been left forever to languish among its fellow ones and zeros on my hard drive.) But it did not take long for a suspicion to form and quickly grow to a certainty: The book didn't need "The Sandmeyer Reaction" anymore!

So I went back to Page 1 of the novel, and made my way through it again, up to this section and then beyond it, all the way to the end. This time I was stalking repercussions, aftereffects and foreshadowings. I was looking for proof that what happened to my protagonist during those mad, painful, absurd 48 hours in Washington and Philadelphia in 1943 was demanded by the emotional or storytelling logic of the events leading up to it. More important, I was looking for evidence that those two days of violence and exaltation burned on, forever afterward, in "my grandfather's" memory. Of course, somewhere inside me, the outcome of my search was already known, or I wouldn't have bothered to conduct it in the first place. By the time I reached the end of the book I didn't have any doubt: Apart from some subsequent gossip among his fellow intelligence officers in Europe about a gangland reputation that has earned him the "Little Caesar"-inspired nickname of Rico, "The Sandmeyer Reaction" was never referred to, directly or indirectly, or thought about, or even avoided as a topic, by any character, at any point in the novel, ever again.

This came as a shock to me, but the remedy was clear enough. Years of planning, months of work, hours of vivid, violent, wakeful dreaming at the keyboard—down the memory hole! Buh-bye, painstaking evocation of a midcentury racetrack backside with its slang and architecture! Buh-bye, creepy, damaged yet oddly tender Lemberger and your sociopathic grace! Buh-bye, days of struggle to concoct a plausible-sounding formula for inadvertently rage-inducing magnetic paint, along with a footnote citing my friend, the real-life chemist Cyrus Harmon, who gave a thumbs up to my guessed-at Sandmeyer reaction!

The Fist of Dread immediately relaxed its grip as I cut away the pages that follow, and the hole they made in the fabric of the book was tellingly small. Two or three sentences needed to be rearranged a bit. I added a paragraph of connective tissue to get my protagonist out of the backwater of Washington, D.C., and into the war in Europe that he is so eager to fight. And that was it. As I stitched up the tiny wound, I had the annoying thought, not at all uncommon at such moments, which are, annoyingly, not at all uncommon: Yeah, I could have told you all along that part was gonna have to go.

By then I knew "my grandfather" well enough to know how he would reply to such arrant kibitzing, and I wish I could repeat his words here but, alas, they are not fit to print. I hope the same can't be said for "The Sandmeyer Reaction." Its surprising isolation from the novel it did so much to shape also gives me hope that it might truly stand on its own, and bring the reader at least as much pleasure as the writing of it, however wasted or misguided, brought to me.

— Michael Chabon

# The Sandmeyer Reaction

**N**ot long before he died, I jotted down the names of the devices and tools my grandfather remembered having contrived during the months he spent working for Stanley Lovell, the OSS's deputy director for special projects, in the basement of a building at 23rd and E. Lovell, a chemist and patent lawyer, had been personally recruited by "Wild Bill" Donovan to equip clandestine operatives in Europe, North Africa, and the Far East. Lovell and his R&D team set to work devising the fountain-pen pistols, lipstick cameras, and cyanide-filled shirt buttons that have since featured in the panoplies of movie and television spies. They found new approaches to infiltration, sabotage, and secret communication. They hit on ways to kill the enemy with cunning and panache, with exploding pancake flour and incendiary bats[*].

The list of my grandfather's devices was fairly long, scrawled with many annotations inside the front cover of the book I happened to be reading that afternoon, Salinger's *Nine Stories*. Decades later, having recommended "For Esmé with Love and Squalor" to my elder daughter, I went looking for *Nine Stories*, one of a number of titles that had been duplicated on the shelves of my first

---

[*] Flying mammals, not sporting gear.

marriage, in graduate school. At the sight of the cover with its grid of colored blocks a memory of the afternoon returned to me: a slant of submarine light through the eucalyptus outside my mother's guest bedroom, my grandfather's brown face against a white pillow, the sound of his Philadelphia vowels at the back of his nose like a head cold. But when I opened the book the inside cover was blank. In making our terminal inventories my ex-wife and I must have exchanged copies. I recall only five of the projects my grandfather claimed to have originated:

1) A crystalline compound, dubbed "whizzite," that when mixed with an operative's own urine, and added to the fuel tank of an airplane, truck or *panzer*, caused delayed but complete and irreparable damage.

2) A small, irregular pyramid of steel that, when wedged against a rail along a stretch of track from which the opposite rail had been loosened—not even removed—was guaranteed to derail any locomotive moving less than 30 mph.

3) A flexible, expandable garrote made of piano wire sheathed in a common shoestring. "Fairly reliable," my grandfather remembered.

4) A pair of "convertible bifocals," the lower half-moons of whose lenses were ground in such a way that with a few twists of the frames they could be arranged to form a serviceable spyglass.

5) A "magnetic paint" that would, for example, permit a limpet mine to be affixed to wood or glass. "That one never quite came together," my grandfather said.

My grandfather had an engineering degree from Drexel Tech, and at first he had found the work interesting, but he was a restless man, prone to confound tedium with rage. He had been trained in subterfuge and violence at a secret base in the Maryland mountains with no mention made of dank basements or chemistry projects. Washington in July was the capital of torpid, and in 1944 the action felt very far away. My grandfather was wild to get into it.

Late one night he was alone in the basement, reading a book and cooking up a fifty-third batch of magnetic paint. The only sounds were the drone of an electric fan and the hiss of the Bunsen jet. The hot night, the string of failures that this batch of magnetic paint would soon extend, the meat grinder into which humanity was feeding itself, and that constant fly-buzz of tedium inside his head all conspired to make my grandfather vulnerable to adventure. He heard what he took to be the sound of someone choking, a man in respiratory distress. He put down his book, stubbed out his cigarette, and went looking, half-intentionally, for trouble.

The office of the deputy director had been improvised in a corner of the basement from book cases and file cabinets dragged from various supply rooms. At the center of this henge Stanley Lovell, an abstemious man not given to demonstrations of emotion, sat slumped in a swivel chair. On the desk in front of him stood a china teacup and an open bottle of Vat 69. His face was red. He dragged a hasty pocket square across his cheeks.

"Tears of anger," he explained.

My grandfather said that in his view they were the only tears worth bothering with.

"George Strong has me by the short ones," Lovell said.

General Strong was the director of the US Army's intelligence service, known as G-2. He and Bill Donovan, director of the rival OSS, loathed each other passionately, and allowed that passion to shape their strategic agendas.

"Now what?" my grandfather said.

My grandfather admired the gallant Donovan but the turf war between OSS and G-2 sickened him. He was contemptuous of pissing contests and tribal loyalties. He despised waste, duplication of effort, the ferocious inertia that prevailed when it was time for OSS to share what it knew with G-2, or G-2 with OSS.

"'Now what?'" Lovell leaned back in the swivel chair and looked up at a steel beam overhead, furred with dust. He spoke in a rapid monotone as though reading from a text printed on the ceiling. "A G-2 informant filed a report claiming that I became intoxicated at a dinner in Georgetown, whereupon I told my companions that the reason Dieppe was a catastrophe was because a German spy passed advance warning through a clue in the Times of London crossword puzzle."

"Dieppe was a catastrophe?" my grandfather said, mildly shocked. German crowing after the failure of the Dieppe raid in 1942 had been widely taken at the time for exaggeration, propaganda. The Allied governments had never said anything to belie this impression.

"Whoops," Lovell said philosophically. He tilted himself forward and smiled at my grandfather without any display of teeth, or humor. He poured another inch of Vat 69 into the teacup, and knocked it back. "That is why I avoid drink. Especially at Georgetown dinner parties."

"So you never said anything at any party. G-2 just wants to smear you."

"Oh, it's nothing personal against me, I'm sure. Strong's just trying to get back at Donovan for Baltimore."

"What happened in Baltimore?"

"Drink or leave, but don't cross-examine me, son. You aren't here to conduct a damn investigation. Sit the hell down."

My grandfather took the other chair. Lovell pushed the bottle across the desk. There was no second teacup or container of any kind. My grandfather wondered if he were meant to drink straight from the bottle.

He went back into the shop, dog-eared a page in his book. A stack of paper cones clung to the side of the water cooler, in a slotted rack. My grandfather took one cone and returned with it to Lovell's office. He lit a cigarette and sipped Vat 69 from the paper cone. He disliked the taste of liquor and disdained its effect on the brain. But there was, after all, a war on.

"What happened in Baltimore is one of our boys was doing his job," Lovell said. "Kid named Quincy, just came out of Area B."

When a class was matriculated from Area B, the OSS training facility, located on the present-day site of Camp David, trainees were subjected to one further test. Each man was provided with a clean suit of clothes, a small amount of cash, and false ID that conferred no special status or authority. He was instructed to make his way to Washington, Baltimore, or Philadelphia, infiltrate a restricted site, and obtain a piece of authentic, useful intelligence.

"So Quincy decides he's going to crack Fort Meade. South of Baltimore."

"What's there?"

"Forty-thousand raw recruits. The Army Cooks and Bakers School. Also, a G-2 training unit. Counter Intelligence Corps."

"Uh-oh."

"Quincy talks his way onto the base. Says he's a reporter for the *Baltimore Sun* doing a story on Fort Meade's security procedures, how incredibly strict they are."

My grandfather employed, and then was obliged to define, the word "chutzpah." He gave the well-known example of the Jew convicted of killing his mother and father who then begged the court to have mercy on a poor orphan. Lovell said he imagined Wild Bill had long since offered that Jew a job.

"Two hours after Quincy gets in the front door at Meade," Lovell went on, splashing another slug into my grandfather's cup, "he is interviewing secretaries in the CIC school front office. Getting all kinds of good stuff, it would appear."

"No one got wise to him?"

"Oh, somebody got wise. A top man of the CIC school could tell our man wasn't kosher, if you'll forgive the expression. Because, in the end, Quincy was a tyro, fresh out of school. He's never infiltrated anything in his life but the girls' cabins on the other side of Lake Wigwam. Unlike the man at the CIC school. Who took Quincy for a spy-hunter. And I suppose that spooked him, because, you see, this particular top man at the CIC school seems to have been a German spy."

"Ah."

"Hence the sense of embarrassment felt at G-2. The tit for which I'm to be the tat."

It was eighty degrees at midnight, ninety-five percent humidity. The smoke from their cigarettes hung in blue swags and coils. The walls perspired. The taste of whisky in my grandfather's mouth was as sluggish and flat as his life and his outlook. Every day in Washington, DC, was a hangover with no preceding spree to justify it. Lovell swung the chair around to a Smith-Corona on a steel typing table beside him. Rolled into its platen was a blank sheet of R&D letterhead darkened by two or three sentences of no great length. He banged out another sentence, hunt-and-peck, pronouncing the words softly as he typed them: *Anxious to bring neither dishonor nor discredit to this agency and to you I must therefore ask you to accept my resignation effective immediately.*

Lovell pulled the sheet out, scanned it, and looked bitterly pleased with what it contained.

"So he got spooked," my grandfather said. "The CIC man."

"He got spooked, he ran. Reportedly to Philadelphia."

"Philadelphia?" my grandfather said. "What part of Philadelphia?"

"You know," Lovell said, tilting back in his chair again to read whatever was written on the ceiling. "I actually am an orphan, just like your fellow with the chutzpah. Parents died when I was a boy. Left my sister and me and not much else."

"Sir?"

"I'm trying to say that I've come very far in life, done very well for myself, without ever being obliged to learn anything about the geography of Philadelphia."

"Tell me this," my grandfather said. He could feel the certainty of salvation or damnation knocking against his rib cage. His life, or at least his war, was at long last about to begin. "Say we grabbed this fella and then handed him over to G–2, let them take the credit for flushing him out, catching him, however they want to play it. All General Strong has to do is drop this Dieppe business and get off your back."

Lovell tilted forward. The hinge of his swivel chair registered his alarm.

"That's the magnetic paint talking," he said. He opened the bottom drawer of his desk and put away the bottle of Vat 69. "The fumes are getting to you."

"Possibly," my grandfather said.

"Who's going to 'grab' him? You?"

My grandfather said that he knew something about the arts of flight and concealment on the streets of Philadelphia. He alluded to certain fellows there, old comrades from boyhood sandlot raids and wars behind the sugar refinery. They had grown up to be tough guys, hoodlums, foot soldiers for men like Nig Rosen and Waxy Gordon. It was their job to fathom the depths of Philadelphia. They might have heard things that policemen and FBI agents were unlikely to hear. As he spoke he saw himself putting a shoulder to the back door of a row house in Gray's Ferry, falling into a roomful of panic and mayhem amid a shower of splinters. He saw himself working his thumbs into the hollow of the German spy's throat. It seemed like it might be fun.

"You're really serious."

"I need to get out of this goddamn basement, sir," my grandfather said. "To be honest."

"Yes, but General Donovan wants you in this goddamn basement. And the last time he didn't get what he wanted was in 1932."[*]

"Give me twenty-four hours." My grandfather looked at his wristwatch, though I remember he always seemed to know within five minutes what time it was. "Midnight tomorrow. Let me try to find the bastard. If I do, you convince Wild Bill to reassign me elsewhere."

"Elsewhere." Lovell's mouth twisted at one corner with what my grandfather presumed must be contempt. "Elsewhere where we're losing an average of five operatives a week? That elsewhere?"

"I'm not picky," my grandfather said. "Any kind of elsewhere will do."

"I did not peg you as the hero type."

"I'm not," my grandfather said, though in fact he believed that he might—perhaps one day very soon—prove to be that very thing. "Just bored."

Lovell shook his head. He looked disappointed in my grandfather. "You're a bright fellow. But I guess not as bright as I thought."

"It's the paint fumes," my grandfather said. "Two weeks ago I was a genius."

Lovell was looking into the teacup as though he hoped to find in it the courage to say no to my grandfather.

"I have to tell you," he said. "There was a mess. After Quincy spooked the man. An exchange of fire. Quincy creased the man's ear, but he got a bullet in the gut for his trouble." He jabbed the barrel of a finger against his stomach. "He almost made it through the debriefing."

---

[*] The year of his unsuccessful bid to succeed FDR as Governor of New York.

My grandfather stood up, and crumpled the paper cone in his fist.

"I'm going to need some Benzedrine," he said. He took his wallet from his hip pocket and made a show of counting the two tens, two fives, and three ones that he had known it to contain. "And two hundred dollars."

Lovell blinked. He looked to be on the point of smiling, but something about my grandfather's expression seemed to discourage him from doing so. He picked up a ring of keys on his desk and went to one of the filing cabinets that entombed him. He unlocked its bottom drawer and took out a steel box painted white and stenciled with a red cross. It was full of wax-paper packets the color of used teabags. He rummaged through them.

"Better not give you the cyanide pills by mistake," he said.

He took out four packets of Benzedrine, four pills to the packet, then went to another file cabinet and unlocked its top drawer. Inside there was a strongbox with a combination lock. Lovell counted out two hundred crisp dollars in tens and fives and passed them to my grandfather along with the pills.

"Hold on," he said.

He opened a door in his desk and brought out a Colt .38 revolver. It was a venerable hunk of iron patched with a nap of dust. It would not have looked out of place on the hip of Teddy Roosevelt, or of Pershing in Mexico. My grandfather weighed it and fingered its grip. He raised it with both hands to take aim at Platinum on a periodic table tacked to the wall. He handed the gun back to Lovell.

"I won't need it," he said.

Lovell followed him out of the maze of filing cabinets to his station. My grandfather shut off the Bunsen burner and switched off the fan. He sat down in a chair by his lab table and took off his black oxfords. He reached under the table for a pair of tan work boots that assorted oddly with his blue serge suit. He slipped his book—it was called *Die Rakete zu den Planetenräumen*—into the hip pocket of his suit jacket. He and Lovell shook hands.

"I used to know when I was making a mistake," Lovell said. "Now I haven't got a clue."

My grandfather went back to his room in the house near Rock Creek Park, took a shower, put on a clean shirt, socks, and necktie. He shaved the blue from his chin and took one of the pills. He caught the first train to Philadelphia from Union Station and with the help of Benzedrine and his ambition organized his thoughts about the best approach to the problem. When he arrived at 30th Street Station in Philly, he found a taxi and directed the driver to the corner of Fourth Street and Ritner.

THE POOL HALL WAS CALLED TIGHE'S, though Tighe was long out of the picture. The present owner, Isidor Mazer, had accepted a majority stake in the establishment as payment for a debt incurred by a nephew of the original Tighe. On a faded wooden sign over the door, half a bisected eight ball dotted the i in "Tighe's." The eight was a token of defeat as well as victory, my grandfather thought, like a roll of seven at craps, or the reckless seizing of what seemed to be opportunity.

Mazer's business, some of it legitimate, was manifold and far-flung. He conducted it from the upstairs room of Tighe's, or at least he had as of the day my grandfather left for Camp Claiborne. Since then Mazer and my grandfather had fallen out of touch.

Their parting had been strained. A beloved older brother of Mazer's had been press-ganged into the Czar's army while still a beardless kid and fed to Japanese Gatlings near the Yalu River in 1905. Mazer's thinking on the subject of military service was muddled by tragedy and rage. When he heard that my grandfather had enlisted he took the news badly. Nevertheless he and his ancient English bulldog, Hadassah, had made my grandfather a little going-away party: a Chinese restaurant, a visit to the best whorehouse in South Philadelphia, and an early-morning run on a Logan Avenue appetizing store. Hadassah, "a prize-winning bitch and the dam of champions," in Mazer's phrase, went everywhere with Mazer. She was wheezy and corpulent in her dotage and looked more like a pig than a dog to my grandfather, who was never especially fond of animals. Her characteristic odor of wet woolen stockings drying on a radiator had not been improved by a plate of creamed herring at Ruby's.

When the party broke up Hadassah and Mazer drove my grandfather down to the train station in Mazer's Model K. Mazer made no effort to restrain his tears.

"Thirteen grand you netted for me," he said. "Just in 1941. With nothing but a wooden stick."

He dabbed at his cheeks with a handkerchief—green, red and gold silk patterned with foxhounds and hunting horns. On the seat beside him sat Hadassah. Thirteen thousand dollars was nothing to Isidor Mazer; he staked my grandfather at pocket billiards not for profit but because he liked to see smiles wiped from the faces of hotshots and fools humiliated. My grandfather said something to this effect.

"Get the fuck out," Mazer said tenderly. He blew his nose into the handkerchief. "You're a smart kid but the Army is going to make you dumb, and then kill you." Hadassah made soft croaking sounds to show that she sympathized. "Good on, get killed, you dumb piece of shit."

That morning in early 1942 the sky had been February gray, the day cold as a nickel. Now it was the gray of August, the morning sticky and warm, a nickel clutched too long in the hand. Tighe's appeared to have gone out of business years before, but there was nothing in that. Mazer's first move on transferring his operation to Tighe's had been to fire the crew that came twice a month to clean the storefront's windows, two big squares gridded with small square panes. A film of grime, smoke, and halitosis municipal and human was permitted to accrue on both sides of the glass. Next Mazer had the fine old etched-glass saloon door with its curlicues of gold-leaf script replaced by plain steel, painted black and fitted with a judas. There were no hours of operation posted, no sign to read open or closed depending on which way you turned it. The brutal geometries of pocket billiards meant as little to Mazer as the men it broke or exalted. He did not care how much business Tighe's did beyond the minimum required to make it a plausible concern in the eyes of tax-gatherers, G-men, and the like.

My grandfather lingered on the sidewalk, contending with a flutter in his stomach. He remembered pausing here to scatter some last-minute butterflies on a muggy evening five years earlier. It was the night of his encounter with Dinky Shavers out of Chicago. He was a kid of nineteen then, his game unknown north of South Street, staked by Isidor Mazer beyond any sum he might ever have hoped to scrape together himself. At that time there had been a store selling layettes on one side of Tighe's, on the other side a dealer in gravestones. It made my grandfather blush to recall having seen something fit, some kind of poetry in that arrangement. Even fifty years later it embarrassed him to admit to having mistaken a case of nerves for foreknowledge of his destiny, between the baby blanket and the shroud, as a pool-room god. Now it was August 1944. He had without regret abandoned his custom Rambow cue, a gift from Mazer on defeating Dinky Shavers, to his kid brother. The gravestone dealer was still in business, but Hirschman's Layette had been replaced by a collection center for scrap metal. And the stirring of fate and poetry in his belly was only Benzedrine.

He took a deep breath. There was a buzzer by the steel door that used to remind him promisingly of a woman's breast, white Bakelite dome, red button. He pushed the nipple twice and let the breath out of his lungs. There was no denying that he had cleaned Dinky Shavers' clock for him that night.

The judas slid open. The expression in the eyes looking over my grandfather wavered between irony and mischief, the eyes of a raccoon ransacking your trash can when you surprised it with a light.

My grandfather recognized the eyes as belonging to Louis Lemberger, a former classmate, even at one time something resembling a friend. Lemberger's father was a chess player, a concert violinist. Until a police horse kicked him in the face while he was watching the 1929 Mummers Parade, Louie Lemberger had been the smartest boy at Thomas Junior High, a whiz kid, self-taught in calculus. The accident left him a mess and an object of universal pity. A story ran in the *Inquirer*, strangers came forward to pay the medical bills. The horse had knocked out almost all of Lemberger's teeth. His nose had been been smashed flat and then poorly reconstructed so that when healed it was larger than before. It looked like the portion of a dressed capon known as the pupik. When he spoke, which happened with increasing rareness, he sounded congested and slow. In time it became apparent that the encounter between his prefrontal cortex and a horseshoe had also knocked loose something in Lemberger's mind. His empirical gifts were bent toward petty arson, cruel pranks, experiments with firecrackers and stray dogs. Within a year he burned off the gas of pity in which the accident had enveloped him. He was still smart but in a way that could be useful only to a man like Mazer.

"I need to see the old man," my grandfather said.

Lemberger said nothing but the irony went out of his gaze leaving only mischief. There was a story from after the accident about Lemberger, a retarded female cousin, and a live mouse. Half a century on my grandfather recalled the story with a shudder and refused to go into it.

The panel in the door began to slide shut.

"Louie, come on. It's important. And I'm in a hurry. Look at this."

My grandfather reached into the breast pocket of his gray suit jacket. Lemberger breathed in sharply, a snuffle of alarm.

"Easy," my grandfather said. "Nice and slow."

He took out the folding sleeve of manila card stock that held his government photostat—his name, an eagle, some digits—and held it up to the judas so that Lemberger could get a look. Lemberger leaned closer. My grandfather raised the manila sleeve half an inch higher. As he followed it with his gaze Lemberger's ruined nose came into view. My grandfather shot out his right hand. He collapsed his fingers together and jammed them through the slot in the door.

Even on an August morning in Philadelphia the flesh of Lemberger's pupik felt strangely clammy. My grandfather hooked his index and middle fingers into Lemberger's nostrils. He clamped down with his thumb. He gave the nose a clockwise twist and pulled it through the slot. Lemberger grunted. He pressed his hands against the door on his side and tried to push back. Something inside the structure of his nose made a sound like celery between the teeth. My grandfather found that he was willing to pull, if necessary, until he pulled the man entire through the slot in the door or the nose tore loose from a red hole in Lemberger's face.

"Open up," he said.

He heard Lemberger scrabbling at the latch. The door swung experimentally inward. My grandfather worked all the strength of his right arm into the pinch-grip of his fingers. As the door opened he saw Lemberger groping in the waistband of his trousers.

My grandfather reached around the door with his left hand and knocked Lemberger's hand away. His fingers closed around the grip of an automatic pistol. It felt as warm and inviting to the touch as Lemberger's nose was repellent and cold. He let go of the nose. Lemberger fell back from the doorway and sat down so hard that his teeth chimed like a pair of castanets. My grandfather was left holding the gun. He stepped into the pool hall with its bouquet of hair oil, and spittoon, and a hint of wool socks drying on a grate. My grandfather shut the door behind him and set the latch. He took the clip out of the gun and slipped it into his pants pocket. He tossed the gun into Lemberger's lap.

"I said I was in a hurry."

At the back of the pool hall a short, narrow flight of stairs led up to Mazer's rooms. When Tighe's was open for business Mazer stationed some professional giant ex-fighter, ex-policeman at the bottom of these stairs. On a busy night there might be two giants, armed with a sap or a knuckleduster, a baseball bat, even a hammer. Mazer saw to it that nobody made trouble. But it was early morning on a weekday and Tighe's was closed. The giants were all home in their giant gatkes sleeping one off. And my grandfather had the magazine from Louis Lemberger's .22 in his pants pocket. If trouble were my grandfather's purpose there was nobody to stop him from making it.

He started for the stairs. Lemberger cursed. He grabbed at my grandfather's right foot in its heavy boot. He got a solid hold on my grandfather's ankle with one hand and pulled. My grandfather was forced to pivot on his left foot but managed not to lose his balance. Lemberger got his other hand around my grandfather's ankle. The cuff of my grandfather's trouser leg rode up. He hopped up and down on his left foot and tried to shake loose of Lemberger.

Lemberger scrambled onto his knees. He pushed his face toward the exposed band of pale leg between my grandfather's cuff and the top of his boot. A half-moon blade cut a slit in Lemberger's face from the inside, just above the chin. It bore a disconcerting resemblance to a smile. My grandfather recalled with a jolt that in close-quarters fighting, Lemberger had been known to rely on the teeth purchased for him years before by kindhearted readers of the *Inquirer.**

My grandfather stopped trying to tug his foot free. He thrust outward with the heel, aiming for the mezzaluna smile. The kick went a little awry. The toe of his boot, reinforced with steel, caught Lemberger between the chin and Adam's apple. Lemberger fell back with his mouth open. He appeared to be screaming, but the only sound that came out was moist and whistling like a garden hose with a pinhole leak. My grandfather rushed the former president of the Thomas Junior High Galileo Club, of which my grandfather had been recording secretary. He raised his foot in its murderous boot. Lemberger opened his eyes wide. My grandfather fought with dwindling resolve against the urge to stomp down on Lemberger's face as hard as he could.

"Knock it off."

My grandfather eased his foot back to the pool hall floor. The cuff of his trouser leg fell into place.

---

* Biting off a convenient part of your enemy in a fight was a venerable South Philadelphia tradition, my grandfather explained, but had always been "more of an Irish thing."

Mazer stood on the stairs in a paisley dressing gown over pin-striped blue pajamas, pale feet stuffed into a pair of black velour mules embroidered with gold anchors. He looked ghastly. The pink plump cheeks had deflated and bore a silvery moire of stretch marks. The pink plump hands had given way to leather over bone. The cancer in Mazer's bowel was not yet public knowledge but my grandfather saw immediately that the old man was done for.[*]

"I have to admit," Mazer said. He reached into the hip pocket of his dressing gown and came up with more than half of a perfecto that he stuck into his mouth. "I'm mildly curious." The cigar bobbed up and down between his teeth.

My grandfather went to Mazer where he was standing haggard on the stairs. He struck a match and held it to the end of Mazer's cigar.

"Say I got shot and needed a doctor to fix me up, but I was intent on keeping a low profile. Would you know who to send me to?"

"Once upon a time, not now," Mazer said. "Such doctors are scarce."

My grandfather felt his throat tighten. He was going to have to do it the hard way now.

"Why is that?" he said.

"A doc willing to do that kind of work, almost by definition he's not going to be your top-drawer practitioner, right? He's a drunk, he killed a patient. Sooner or later he's going to perform malpractice on somebody, amputate the wrong leg or something.

---

[*] He died on April 12, 1945, the same day as FDR.

The kind of clientele he serves have a violent way of taking their business elsewhere."

"So who *would* know, if you don't? Who can I ask for a referral?"

"Asking what? Asking for who? What are we talking about here?"

"I'm going to need a doctor," my grandfather said.

Mazer crossed his eyes and smacked his lips until the cigar caught fire. He held it up between two wasted fingers and watched the flame dwindle to a rippled thread of smoke.

"You're *going* to need a doctor," he said.

He stuck the cigar back into his mouth. He blew a gust of smoke into my grandfather's face.

His blue eyes were as bright and irritable as ever. He brushed past my grandfather and shuffled in his slippers to the "Throne of Elijah," a wingbacked chair with a needlepoint footrest and a view of the best table, where the big money changed hands.

"Why?" he said.

"Gunshot wound."

Mazer frowned. He looked my grandfather up and down appraisingly but with a reluctant shake of the head as though to stipulate ahead of time that he knew my grandfather was putting him on. My grandfather heard Lemberger behind him, a scrape of leather sole against the parquet floor. He reached into the pocket of his suit jacket. He fingered the clip he had taken from Lemberger's gun.

"Yeah?" Mazer said. "Who's going to shoot you?"

Without looking behind him my grandfather tossed the clip over his left shoulder. There was a slap, metal against palm, neat as the arc of a nice catch.

"Lemberger," said my grandfather.

ONE THING I THOUGHT I KNEW was that at some Moonblatt wedding of the late 1960s my grandfather had presented me to a dapper old party whose name was Dr. Fireman. This Dr. Fireman wore a white Panama hat and a knotted foulard. His Buster Browns were Steinway black. A gold watch chain described a transatlantic route across the globe of his belly.

In spite of the man's panache and beguiling surname I might well have forgotten him, along with all the other guests at the reception that evening. But from the moment my grandfather led me into the room—some banquet hall in the wilderness of Levittown—I understood that to my grandfather Dr. Fireman was a person of mysterious importance. My grandfather crouched down beside me, put an arm around my shoulder, and pointed out the silver-haired dandy in a pinstriped double-breasted suit, sitting lonely as a mountain in a corner of the room.

"Come," he said. "Let's give the man a look at you."

Afterward I would forget whatever passed between Dr. Fireman and me in the way of conversation, but I kept the distinct impression that the old man had been pleased to meet me. When after two minutes he and I parted company forever I was in dazzled possession of a Liberty dollar as heavy and venerable as history itself.

Only, it turned out, I had it all wrong. It wasn't a wedding or a Moonblatt affair; the old man's name was not Fireman; and he wasn't a doctor at all.

"It was Artie Newman's bar mitzvah," my grandfather said. He had slept more soundly than usual during the night. On waking he had asked for French toast, which he called "Pan Purdoo" in the exaggerated tourist-from–Iowa accent he put on whenever he said something in French. His voice was strong and his color less sallow. I knew he would never recover but seeing pink in his cheek and hearing a bass note in his voice I could not help thinking that he might. "The guy's name was Feuerman. He was a horse trainer, his horses won a lot of races. He was a friend of Marvin Marx."

That was a name I hadn't heard in a while, one always charged, in my family, with a certain dark romance. Marvin Marx was something to my cousin Artie on his mother's side, no blood relative of mine. He was an attorney with ties to the Bruno crime family. (The atmospherics of his career had inspired certain elements of the plot of my first novel.) When casino gambling came to Atlantic City in the late seventies, it was Marvin Marx, people said, who did the lawyering.

When the mob bosses of Philadelphia went to war—I was a senior in high school at the time— Marvin Marx disappeared while on vacation in Hollywood, Florida. It later emerged that he had been shot and strangled by unknown persons who expertly dismembered him, packed him in pieces into a steel oil drum, and sank the oil drum in fifty feet of water off Key Biscayne.

Neglecting to consult my grandfather, who had no connection whatever to the matter but would have been happy to explain the biochemistry of putrefaction, the killers failed to punch the necessary escape holes in the oil drum. A month after Marx's disappearance it bobbed to the surface of Biscayne Bay and its place in family lore.

"Feuerman had ties, too," my grandfather said. "On a lot of those horses of his, I heard it was really Angelo Bruno who put up the money."

"But..." I tried to square this information with the dollar-sized memory I'd been clutching all those years. "But you called him 'Doctor.'"

"No," my grandfather said, "I called him 'Doc.' It was a little joke we had."

LEMBERGER SHOT MY GRANDFATHER with the .22, at close range, aiming for a part of the body with no bones or vital organs—the one known to later decades as a "love handle." The slug drilled a hole in my grandfather from front to back and lodged in the ornate frame of a portrait of John L. Sullivan, where it remained until 1972, when the building that housed Tighe's was torn down, prompting a eulogy by *Philadelphia Daily News* columnist Tom Fox. According to local legend, Fox wrote, the stray shot "was the parting gift of a Nazi spy on the lam." As with the silvery asterisk on my grandfather's ass left behind by the teeth of a broken bottle, a pair of faint white blazes fore and aft forever commemorated the path of Lemberger's bullet*. The wound was clean and well executed but it bled freely and burned like hot wire.

"For Christ's sake," said Isidore Mazer from the comfort of the "Throne of Elijah." "You didn't say you were planning to make such a goddamn mess."

Mazer had once worked as a cutman for Lew Tendler. He knew his way around a needle driver and suture thread, and had already offered, more than once, to patch my grandfather up. It galled him to see my grandfather stand there bleeding all over the floor of his pool hall, not to mention ruining a perfectly good handkerchief.

"Silk," Mazer said. "Twelve dollars at Strawbridge and Clothier."

"Put it on my tab," my grandfather said. He felt that for the sake of authenticity it would have to appear that he had made shift to dress his wound himself.

He bit through the whipstitched hem of the silk handkerchief and then tore it in half. He reached around and tried to poke one of the halves with exceeding gentleness into the exit wound. Lightning forked across his back. His resolve faltered and the bit of handkerchief popped loose from the hole. My grandfather just managed to catch it before it could fall to the ground.

---

* The first time I noticed these scars, as a kid, my grandfather told me that when he was stationed at Camp Lejeune a "bayou worm" had bored its way into his abdomen. He said that the bayou worm had laid hundreds of eggs that gestated for three years before emerging, through a hole in his back, in a painful cavalcade of worms that lasted five hours. The inquiry was never repeated.

He swore, and then turned his attention to the entry wound, which naturally was easier to get at. He took a breath and set his jaw. This time when he worked in the piece of handkerchief lightning flickered all the way to the roots of his eyeballs. His legs bowed and then seemed to forget their business entirely. Lemberger stepped forward to grip him by the elbow.

"Steady," he said.

The moment my grandfather asked Lemberger to put a bullet through his midsection the animosity between them had been forgotten. Lemberger seemed to have gained new respect for my grandfather, not as a man who would let himself be shot for the sake of verisimilitude but as an unexpected source of entertainment.

"How about I do the back for you?" Lemberger said.

"If you wouldn't mind," said my grandfather.

He pasted his fingers to the exit wound and waited while Lemberger went to a small basin that was bolted to the wall outside the toilet. He ran hot water and washed his hands carefully with the castile soap that Mazer provided. Every psychopath he ever knew, my grandfather told me—he put the number at five—had been dependably hygienic.

While he waited for Lemberger to finish washing, my grandfather took measured breaths. He reminded himself that the difference between pain and pleasure was subjective, a matter of context. No doubt there were people out there who would enjoy getting holed by a .22. He tried to imagine that he was that kind of person.

"So where did I go?" my grandfather asked Mazer. "Who's going to know the doc that'll fix me up no questions asked?"

"*Now* you ask me that?" Mazer said. "What if the answer's 'nobody'? What if I say I don't know?"

"I asked you before."

Mazer shook his head. He quoted, not for the first time, a wise proverb he claimed to have once found inside of a fortune cookie: "The journey of a thousand miles begins by leaving out a crucial step."

"But I told you what the plan was going to be," my grandfather said.

"Yes," Mazer said. "And as you may recall I attempted to dissuade you from it."

My grandfather felt the edge of something cold and cutting laid against his scalp at the hairline. It was the cooling of his sweat. He felt like he might want to vomit, but there would be no point, since he had eaten nothing for the past several hours but Benzedrine pills. So he forbore.

"'What if the answer's nobody?'" Lemberger said. He jerked some fresh towel down from the roll dispenser and blotted his hands. "That's hysterical." He didn't laugh. "Now then."

My grandfather passed Lemberger the other half of the handkerchief and pulled his hand from the wound. There was a peeling sound as his fingers came unstuck.

Lemberger's fingers were again briefly five iron cuffs along my grandfather's arm. Then somebody tripped a circuit breaker in my grandfather's head, and he was plunged into darkness.

When the lights came on again Lemberger was hugging my grandfather from behind, holding him up by the armpits. The toes of my grandfather's boots just grazed the floor. Mazer was standing right in front of him, peering in at my grandfather's face like an exterminator checking a baseboard for holes. The whites of Mazer's eyes were something closer to ivory. Under the bouquet of his eau de cologne there was something rancid, a bit of meat left between the teeth overnight.

"Tell me what this is already," Mazer said. "Enough."

My grandfather worked himself loose of Lemberger. He saw to it that his legs remembered why he kept them around.

"If I could tell you, Iz, I swear to you, I would."

"Show me the piece of paper that you showed to Louis," Mazer said.

The government identification card in its folded manila sleeve did not give very much away but after he had glanced at it and turned it over once or twice Mazer seemed to feel that he had a better grasp of the situation. He went back over to the wingbacked chair. On his way he fished a dime from the pocket of the paisley robe.

Next to the "Throne of Elijah" sat a primitive Wurlitzer jukebox, made of fumed oak. It had a window leafed with gold curlicues and when you looked in the window you saw twelve shellac records, racked like drying dinner plates. Only Mazer was allowed to operate this piece of equipment, and he only ever played one song, "Stars Fell on Alabama." All the other records were what my grandfather called "blue." They had been selected by previous management and had titles like "Banana in Your Fruit Basket" and "Meat Balls." Mazer was a prude. He hated that stuff. The only reason he kept the jukebox around was to have the satisfaction of forbidding its use to others.

Mazer pressed the button for "Stars Fell on Alabama" and lowered himself onto his throne. A shaft turned a cam, a cam drove a wheel that moved a belt. A metal pawl ticked against a ratchet. Guy Lombardo's orchestra started to play.

"Twenty years ago, I could've referred you to three, four crooked docs myself," Mazer said. "Truly it was an age of gold."

"Albert the Chink?" Lemberger said. He was digging around in a cabinet under the cash register. This cash register was of an even earlier vintage than the jukebox. It had never in my grandfather's experience been used to hold money or ring up a charge. Mazer liked to keep accounts in his head and cash out of view. He felt that the sight of money like the bare flesh of a woman interfered with men's ability not to be idiots. "He has the eyes, but he's a Yid." At the back of the cabinet Lemberger found a box of rolled gauze. "His brother's some kind of doc. I had to go to him to get tested for the Medicine merit badge."

It came back to my grandfather, painful in a different way: Louie Lemberger with a kerchief around his neck. The tan shorts, the high woolen socks.

"Albert the Chink's brother has a permanent case of the shakes, Baden-Powell," Mazer said. "He lives under the Girard Avenue Bridge. He couldn't sew up a chicken."

My grandfather waved away the roll of gauze that Lemberger proffered.

"It'll look better if I don't bandage it. Like I was in more of a rush."

"Say you swiped it from a drugstore." The damage that had been done to Lemberger's face by a policeman's horse at the Mummers parade seemed momentarily to worsen. "Say you jumped a nurse."

My grandfather recoiled. The way Lemberger came out with the nurse scenario was a little too vivid. But he had to acknowledge that bleeding to death might get in the way of the job he was trying to do. He took off his bloody shirt and allowed Lemberger to mummify his abdomen. Lemberger did the job with precision worthy of a merit badge.

"Pelz?" Lemberger said over his shoulder, talking to Mazer. He pressed the end of the gauze bandage against the outcrop of my grandfather's hip with the fingers of his right hand. "Turn. Keep turning."

"Why did I think Pelz was dead?" Mazer said.

"So he is," Lemberger said. "My mistake."

"The guy at the mick funeral home on Taney."

"Doyle."

"Not Doyle."

"Doyle."

"Is that Doyle?"

"He went in the Navy."

"Funny how they do the open casket and we don't," Mazer said. "No wonder people don't trust us."

"How do you figure?"

"I mean, open the goddamn casket," Mazer suggested to their fellow Jews around the world. "What are you trying to hide?"

My grandfather had considered that risk of death would increase with the period of time between gunshot and treatment, but in his planning he had failed to take into account, among other things, the established fact that for unknown reasons no conversation at Tighe's Pool Room, no matter how pea brained, had ever lasted less than three hours. He hoped that packing and binding the wounds would keep him from bleeding to death before these two managed to come up with the name of someone who was likely to know a doctor sufficiently ruined to treat criminals and German spies on a clandestine cash basis.

"Talking of Catholics," Lemberger said. "There's that priest. Ex-priest. The one that taught science at Southeast Catholic."

"Monk."

"Ex-monk. He used to run a hospital in Camden. He's got to know a lot of docs. He's a Polack."

"Hungarian."

"Hungarian?"

"How about we get out the phone book," my grandfather said. "Go through it name by name under 'Crooked Doctor Referral'?"

Mazer and Lemberger looked up at my grandfather with expressions of mild surprise.

"I for one have reached the limits of my ignorance," Mazer said. "I would apologize, but this situation is hardly my fault."

"I can give you a lift over to the Girard Avenue Bridge if you want to look for Albert the Chink's brother," Lemberger said.

My grandfather picked up his bloody shirt, tweezing it at the shoulder seams with his fingertips. When he put the shirt back on it felt cold and stiff against his skin.

"I told you the war would make you stupid," Mazer said. "I warned you. Two years ago you would never have let Lemberger shoot you for nothing."

"It wasn't for nothing," Lemberger said. "Now he knows how it feels to get shot."

Mazer made one of the rueful snorting noises that served him for laughter, but Lemberger did not appear to have been joking, which my grandfather appreciated. If he were to make it through this fucked-up situation alive, he thought, then being shot would be one less thing to waste time worrying about. Being shot turned out to be like everything else that happened in life: either it killed you or it didn't. The same odds obtained across the board, with or without gunplay: at the end of every day you were either alive, or you weren't. Every day, death paid even money. He didn't regret having let Lemberger shoot him. What bothered him was that now the Nazi was going to get away with killing Quincy, and General Strong was going to hand Stanley Lovell his ass, and maybe Wild Bill his, while he was at it. And my grandfather would never escape the torpor of Washington, the basement at 23rd and E. Once again the start of the life he was destined to lead would have to be postponed. It was too bad the war had made him stupid.

"Stitch me up, then," he told Mazer. "As long as I don't die in this dump."

Before Mazer could say anything smart there was a chiming from the stairwell at the back of the pool room. A series of hammer taps alternated with drum-kicks as Hadassah fell slowly and with a show of dignity down the stairs. When the dog hit bottom she slid her hindquarters under her belly, deftly, a waiter helping a fat man onto a seat cushion. She gave out a wheeze of pleasure. It had been a long and arduous journey from her spot by the gas fire in Mazer's office. She grinned at Mazer. Black lips, pink tongue, teeth the color you found inside a cotton cigarette filter after you had smoked the cigarette. Gulping air with that sound like she had a permanent head cold. She was leathern and bloated, the offspring of a set of bagpipes and a medicine ball. My grandfather estimated that on that morning in 1944 she must have been at least twenty years old.

"Hold on a second, now," Mazer said. He was talking to my grandfather, but he was looking at the dog. "Wait. Don't die yet."

MY GRANDFATHER GOT INTO LEMBERGER'S CAR, a '38 Pontiac coupe, rolled down the window, and passed out. There was nothing after that until something cold and hard nuzzled the hollow of his ear.

"Wake up, peaches," Lemberger said.

My grandfather started awake and the sudden motion lit up the bullet holes. The pain was bad but on the other hand it was in its way comforting because in the half-second before it hit my grandfather could not remember where he was or what he had come there to do. A shudder rippled through his body. The thing nuzzling his ear turned out to be the snout of Lemberger's gun. My grandfather batted it away.

"Take it," Lemberger said. He had stopped the car and cut the engine. "You want it. Go on."

"No thanks."

Lemberger misunderstood.

"I got others," he said. "This is just my little Tuesday morning breakfast gun."

He pressed the gun into the palm of my grandfather's left hand. My grandfather fought an impulse to jerk the hand away. His skin revolted against the chill of it and another shudder whip-cracked through him. He could not shake the sensation of the cold muzzle against his ear, which somehow he was also experiencing as a taste of metal at the back of his tongue. He forced his fingers to close around the waffle-iron of the pistol grip. He worked to pull himself together.

"Okay?" Lemberger said.

"Okay."

"Yeah?"

"Yeah."

That was a lie; he had never felt so profoundly wrong. It was like when you fell asleep in a funny position and woke up with someone else's arm in the bed with you, attached to your shoulder. Only this was not just an arm, it was his whole body that felt like somebody else's. He decided to try looking out the car window to see if that helped.

They were parked on the shoulder of a stretch of unpainted blacktop alongside a whitewashed fence. Beyond the fence lay a meadow. The morning smelled of wet grass and something heavier, some tree in flower, a fecund smell that verged on rottenness. Across the road there was another green meadow behind another white fence, more trees. At the moment there were no horses in view, but horses were definitely implied. This was DuPont country, somewhere outside of Wilmington, Delaware. DuPonts would have horses.

"It hurts."

"A well-known fact about getting shot."

"Not that." My grandfather pointed at the meadow. "That."

He could not explain. The white was too radiant, the green too ripe. The black loops drawn by bees among the grass blades seemed to pick at my grandfather like sutures. A red horse came up over a rise at the far end of the meadow. My grandfather supposed the word for that color of horse was bay. The sky behind the horse was heavy and luminous with rain. Even at a distance the red of the horse's coat against the gray, to my grandfather, was like sandpaper against the skin. He wondered if getting shot had addled him, or if his recent attempt to confound pain with pleasure had broken something in his brain.

"Yeah," Lemberger said. "Fucking bastards."

Even though Lemberger was a psychopath, and even though at that moment my grandfather was unconcerned with the dialectics of class struggle, he knew what Lemberger meant. They were poor boys, the sons of socialists who revered Heywood and voted Debs. The pretty meadow and the white fence belonged to a man who was likely to rate that bay horse more highly than he would ever have rated my grandfather, Lemberger, or anyone who came from their world.

For a moment they watched the rich man's horse rummage and rip at the grass up at the top of the rise. It moved slant-foot across the meadow with a sneaking laziness like a shortstop cheating in on a runner at second. To my grandfather's eye it had been foolishly or fancifully engineered to defy harsh laws of gravity and dynamics, a cathedral built to stand upon its steeple.

"Thoroughbred," Lemberger said.

"Yeah?"

"Yeah. All this, it's stud farm."

It seemed unlikely Lemberger would not follow this observation with something lewd but it was quiet enough in the coupe to hear the bees stitching up the dandelions.

"You ever ride a horse?" my grandfather said.

"Once," Lemberger said. "But I only rode its hoof."

"Christ, Lou. I'm sorry."

"You're sorry?"

"I should have thought."

"You know, horses come up in conversation from time to time. I almost never faint anymore."

"I know it's belated," my grandfather said. He was aware that after fourteen years this was possibly an understatement. "It was rotten what happened to you."

"Think I give a shit if you're sorry, ass-rag?"

"I would be disappointed if you did."

"Anyway I must have deserved it," Lemberger said. "Otherwise it wouldn't have happened, right?"

My grandfather said that was a question with two sides and he could see them both, and Lemberger said that was perfect for a guy with a hole on two sides of his body. Then he reached into the Pontiac's backseat for a gray London Fog raincoat that had been forgotten in the pool room years ago.

"Put this on," he said. "You'll walk right in."

My grandfather took the coat and the gun and got out of the car. The raincoat was too long and tight at the shoulders but it covered the bloody shirt. It was a piece of luck that rain clouds had blown in during the ride down from Philly but my grandfather did not mistake this for an omen of success. For the time being at least he was cured of that type of thinking. The truth was he had given up hope of catching the German spy, any German spy, now or at any time in his life to come. In Lovell's office he had thought he was holding one end of a chain of unbreakable inferences:

1) The fugitive would seek treatment for his injury.

2) He would be obliged to do so *sub rosa*.

3) Doctors willing to provide such services were few and hard to find, even in Philadelphia, but

4) Isidor Mazer would know where to send my grandfather.

5) Given the scarcity of back-alley sawbones, there was a decent chance that the one my grandfather went to would also have treated the spy, and would—if left alive— be able to give my grandfather a notion of the fugitive's current whereabouts or next destination.

But it had all broken down at 4) and once again the thing my grandfather had taken for the unfurling of a plan had turned out to be nothing but a spasm of impulsiveness. When he got back to Washington he was going to have to take a closer look at the military value of magnetic paint. Apparently it possessed the power to induce delusions of grandeur*.

My grandfather shut the door and stepped back from the car. He dropped the pistol into a pocket of the raincoat.

"So," he said, abruptly tired. "Where do I go?"

"Service road."

Lemberger pointed. About fifty yards down from where they were parked a narrower road branched off to the left. A white fence accompanied it but then appeared to give up and turn back as though in distaste or despair just before the service road entered some trees. Beyond and above the screen of trees my grandfather could see an elegant sweep of green roof, a streaming pennant.

"You think he really was here?"

"Fuck no," Lemberger said. "Do you?"

"I dunno. The guy told Mazer."

"Some guy told Mazer maybe some other guy heard something about somebody's nephew that someone else might maybe have seen. How much more than bupkis is that?"

"Not very much," my grandfather conceded.

---

* In the OSS Archives at the Library of Congress, I found photostat copies of some notebooks taken from Lovell's laboratory. According to Cyrus Harmon, a chemist at Olema Pharmaceuticals, to whom I showed the photostats, one route attempted in my grandfather's effort to produce a "magnetic paint" involved the synthesis of aryl halides by means of a Sandmeyer reaction. Though the notes do not specify which reagent was employed, among the most common is the compound $CH_3(CH_2)_4ONO_2$, better known as amyl nitrite, or "poppers."

In the mid-1930s a horse trainer from Camden, New Jersey, had come to Mazer with a business proposition. The horse trainer's mother had a sister who was married to a Teamster who was married to a sister of Mazer's. A veterinary school dropout who had served as an Army muleteer in Panama, the horse trainer now worked the ovals and backsides of the mid-Atlantic circuit, supplementing his income by doctoring escapees and gunsels. In this secondary trade he had a certain reputation. It was said that one of his proprietary poultices had saved "Little Krissy" Herman from the otherwise fatal effects of a poisoned slug. He was tired of tending to other men's horses, he told Mazer, and there was a yearling grandson of Broomstick he had his eye on. But he lacked the necessary funds. He had spotted a few flaws in the way things were done at Freehold Racecourse, and a way of exploiting them. He bided his time watching for the other required elements to present themselves: two all but indistinguishable horses, one a game young unknown and one a career also-ran. Then he went to Mazer for the necessary yiches. Documents and ear tattoos were altered, bribes were pocketed, and the impostor came in at 30- to-1. Mazer was so pleased that he sent the horse trainer a reward: a pup from a recent litter of Hadassah's. That was the cue Hadassah had provided when she came downstairs to see what the fuss was about.

After the switcheroo things had unraveled a bit for the horse trainer. Only a month after he acquired Broomstick's grandson an exerciser who had taken his breakfast from a shot glass fell off the yearling during a routine warm-up and got tangled in the animal's legs. When the mess got untangled the man was dead and the animal had to be destroyed. There were whispers of investigations planned by certain unbribed elements of the state regulatory system. The horse trainer had thought it prudent to hit the road. Iz Mazer had not seen him again until a few weeks ago, when he turned up at Bookbinder's, having dinner with some touts and cheap gamblers.

Mazer had assumed then that the horse trainer was only home for a visit, but on the other hand the Teamster father had recently run off with a cocktail waitress at the Hotel Sylvania, leaving the mother bedridden. A devoted son might have come home to stay, and perhaps taken up his wonted means of support. The horse trainer might very well be the only man in the Greater Philadelphia area at this moment who could provide the kind of quiet and the level of competence that my grandfather's quarry required. So Mazer had made a telephone call from his office at Tighe's. Dots were connected. There were not quite enough dots to make a picture, but it was better than rousting some rummy under the Girard Avenue Bridge.

"Happy hunting," Lemberger said.

He started the engine, pulled away from the shoulder, and turned the Pontiac around. My grandfather watched until he was sure he had been abandoned to his work. Wrong as Lemberger might be in the head, my grandfather felt nothing but pity toward him, and so it was a great relief to see him go. My grandfather thought he might be feeling a bit steadier now. He patted at the bandage. It felt damp but not soaked in blood. He was probably still in shock but at least the nausea and the sense of bodily dislocation seemed to have passed. He was hungry, now— famished; that too must be a positive sign. On balance he would have preferred not being shot, but he was glad at least to have again put Philadelphia behind him.

The grass rustled. He heard what he took for a sigh of irritation. He fished the .22 from the raincoat pocket and spun around, feeling a jolt that was only part panic; the rest of it was pure eagerness to shoot.

The red horse was standing at the fence looking sidelong at him with a dark, flirtatious eye. Shifting light veneered its chest, and tendons stood out from the scrollwork of its legs. My grandfather could see the energy strung along the cords of its musculature, could almost hear the music it held in tension, waiting to be struck. But it was his heart that resounded. Looking at the red horse he felt its beauty pulling at something inside him that he would rather have died than call his soul, drawing that nonexistent organ out of his body like the interplanetary soul of Capt. John Carter of Virginia at the start of *A Princess of Mars*.

He slipped the gun back into his pocket.

"For now," he told the red horse. "But if nobody down there gives me any breakfast I'm coming back to eat you."

The red horse lowered its head to address its own breakfast. It gave its tail a twitch. It didn't say anything in reply but my grandfather understood perfectly well that he was to go fuck himself.

PASSING THROUGH THE LITTLE STAND OF TREES toward the backside of Delaware Park he heard horses bugling. Breakfast time for everyone. When he stepped out of the trees the horses, all at once, left off. The morning seemed to hold its breath. Just as my grandfather began to feel unnerved by the sudden silence the rain started, and a moment later the horses resumed their complaint.

The fence here was steel post and hurricane mesh whip stitched along the top with barbed wire. Where it met the road there was a steel gate and a kind of hut with a folding chair inside. The gate stood wide open but you would never get through it without first getting past the man sitting in the hut. Just inside the gate a horse trailer foundered in a surf of mud. Opposite the capsized trailer rose a hump of horse dung wreathed in steam. Beyond the gate the road dissolved in mud and was lost amid a jumble of trailers, canvas tents, shacks, cabins, and dozens of long white structures that looked like barracks but were, my grandfather guessed, the horse barns. Some of the buildings were painted white or gray or brick red, others were innocent of paint. The barns had green roofs to match the grandstand's and were clad in board-and-batten, but the rest of the backside buildings were roofed in rolled creosote or sheets of corrugated metal nailed down at three corners out of four. Some of the structures were no more than tarpaper tacked up over a frame of two-by-fours. It looked as if a traveling circus and a hobo jungle had thrown in with an army boot camp to see how much open land they could cover if they pooled their resources. You could still make out traces of some original plan; the horse barns were laid out in orderly ranks. But everything else appeared to have been stranded by receding floodwaters or dumped here one building at a time, much the worse for wear, by passing tornadoes. The grandstand with its flags and gingerbread porches did not so much rise behind this encampment so much as fall athwart it, rung down like a theater curtain painted with a fairy-tale scene.

The man sitting in the little three-sided hut had some coals going in an overturned hubcap set on some bricks by his feet. Across the hubcap lay a piece of steel mesh of the kind used to cover the windows of prison buses. As my grandfather approached the gate the man was poking with a long fork at five fat paprika-colored sausages he had arranged on the piece of steel mesh. The sausages did not appear to be anywhere near ready, but the man had already tucked a handkerchief into his shirt collar and spread it over his shirtfront. His heavy Redwings had a fresh shine and much less mud caked on their soles than might have been expected. His chambray shirt was crisp and the creases down the front of his brown ducks were yardstick true. The rolled sleeves of his shirt allowed glimpses of tattoos; on the left arm it said PROVERBS 26:3 but on the right arm all my grandfather could see was the bottom edge of a billowing banner done in blurred green-black ink and the feet of some letters that might turn out to say ROSALIE or HELLBOUND. The man wore his black hair long in front and combed romantically back in the style of Frankie Sinatra, but his brush mustache suggested an officious nature and my grandfather sensed he might be in for a hard time. The man was evidently irritated with the dilatory sausages and when he looked up from the grill to my grandfather the expression on his face stayed the same.

"I'm looking for Feuerman," my grandfather said.

The man ran an eye up and down the raincoat. It appeared to raise doubts in his mind. The pattering rain hissed as it hit the fire. The man held up the barbecue fork. Like the brazier it was a kind of contraption, improvised by poking an old shrimp cocktail fork into the coiled spring at one end of those wands you mounted on an ironing board to keep the cord of the iron from getting in your way. The man lifted an eyebrow. The expression on his face changed now to suggest both menace and amusement. You must now prepare yourself, the expression said, to be prodded with a very long fork.

The man reached out, slowly, explicitly, his eyes keeping steady contact with my grandfather's. The tines of the fork aimed for the left pocket of the raincoat. Just before it made contact there the man's eyebrow went up even higher. He was toying with my grandfather, openly and in a way that my grandfather found mildly hypnotic. The fork jerked and then veered like a dowsing rod toward the right pocket where it found the bulge of the .22. Gently the trident tap-tapped.

"Okay," my grandfather said. "Easy."

He tweezed the gun out of the pocket and held it pinched like an old sock between two fingers, to emphasize its uselessness to him. The man angled the fork upward so that the little trident was pointed at the gun. He waggled the fork suggestively.

"It might be too heavy."

The man gave the fork another waggle. My grandfather fitted the gun over it, feeding the tines through the space between the trigger and the trigger guard. Then he let go of the gun. The wire wand bowed, deep, but did not dip, and then sprang back as the gun slid along it toward the man's hand. He switched the fork to his left hand and let the gun fall off it at the bottom into the palm of his right. The callouses on his palm where it met the fingers were thick and lustrous as tortoiseshell. He emptied the chamber and pocketed the bullets with a touch of legerdemain, pausing only to glance up at my grandfather when he noted that the bullets numbered five. He passed the gun back to my grandfather, who shook his head.

"I don't want it."

The man took in this new information. He set the gun down on a little shelf inside the hut, between a roll of Sen-Sen and a pouch of Drum.

"This ain't no fire station," he said.

It took my grandfather a few seconds to understand.

"Not 'fireman,'" he said. "Feuerman."

"Uh huh. You know this ain't no fuckin' hospital neither."

Then he reached out again with the fork. This time he aimed for the raincoat's bottommost button. My grandfather looked down at the front of the raincoat. The fabric was beaded with quicksilver droplets of rain but was not, it appeared, impermeable to blood. There was a dark blotch shaped roughly like the island of Ceylon over his right side. The man poked at the bottom button. Deftly and with a criminal √©lan he worked the shrimp fork into the buttonhole and over the top of the button till the thing popped open. Moving upward he made short work of popping the uppermost buttons. When the coat fell open he used the fork to lift aside the right flap of the raincoat. What he saw was nothing mysterious or hard to interpret.

"Christ." He let the flap fall back into place. "What happened there, boss?"

"I was bitten by an ocelot."

The man hid a smile up under the nailbrush he had growing from his upper lip and returned his attention to the cook fire. He stabbed at a sausage. The fork that had acquitted itself so well with pistols and coat buttons displayed certain shortcomings when applied to its intended task. The sausages rolled around on the grate trying to escape their fate. The man leaned down, trying to gain leverage, and the closer he got, the more the wire bowed and flexed. It took several tries and a certain amount of cursing before he managed to spear one of the sausages. He lifted it to his nose and took an appreciative whiff.

"Mr. Mazer sent me," my grandfather said. "Isidor Mazer."

The words emerged from his throat freighted with a great deal more desperation than he had intended or even necessarily known that he felt. Rain was pooling inside his ears and at the small of his back. The bullet wounds throbbed asynchronously, in and out of phase, so that he could never anticipate and thus get on top of the pain that had, he was at last forced to concede, nothing at all to do with pleasure whatsoever. His head was light and his stomach empty. And the sausage smelled wonderful.

The man ate it in three bites, watching my grandfather. Mazer's name appeared to have made no impression on him. A pickup truck rolled up the gate, its bed mounded with sawdust. It was driven by a diminutive elderly Negro wearing a wide-brimmed hat of woven straw. The word MEXICO was embroidered in red thread on the crown. There were holes cut into the brim on either side as if to accommodate the ears of a horse or possibly a mule. The stall man and the driver of the truck, whose name or nickname appeared to be Mexico, engaged in banter about some aspect of work or politics in the backside that my grandfather found at once distracting and incomprehensible. Then the truck rolled away through the gate and when my grandfather looked back the man's mustache was shining and there was only one sausage left on the grate.

The air between my grandfather and the stall man was abruptly swarming with sparkling points of light. My grandfather thought that the drops of rain were catching a patch of sun at a strange angle. He had heard the expression "seeing stars" used with reference to lightheadedness but he had never understood that it described an actual phenomenon. In cartoons when people were about to faint or had been knocked silly a halo of stars (if not little birds) would orbit their heads but this too had seemed to be purely convention like the Xs cartoon corpses had for eyes.

He had the odd sensation that the water filling his shoes was not rain but blood, streaming down from his head, not from his wounds. The stall man cursed, bending down and jabbing at the last sausage as the wand buckled and the shrimp fork wiggled in the spring coil.

"You ought to use a telescoping aerial," my grandfather said. "You could adjust the length depending on how much leverage you needed. If you could shorten it then it would also make it easier to eat with."

The stall man stopped trying to stab the sausage and looked at my grandfather.

"Huh," he said.

In spite of the fact that he was now tottering at the edge of unconsciousness my grandfather briefly outlined six improvements that he would make to the design of the stall man's barbecue fork, including attaching the fork to the aerial with a metal collar and a rivet and adding a simple grip at the other end, using the handle from an old trowel or a piece cut from a broomstick.

"You talk like an engineer," said the stall man.

My grandfather said that there was a good reason for this. He gave a brief sketch of his career up to the meeting with Wild Bill. The stall man started to grin before my grandfather was halfway through the account. When my grandfather ran out of things to say or the strength to say them the stall man pushed up the sleeve of his left arm to display the tattoo. The motto in the banner was not ROSALIE or HELLBOUND but the French imperative ESSAYONS. Over the banner, executed very poorly, was the heraldic castle with four turrets that symbolized the Army Corps of Engineers.

"I guess I'm going to have to let you have this fucking sausage," the stall man said. He succeeded in spearing it, but just as he raised it off the grate and began to swing it toward my grandfather there was a sound of wheezing and huffing. My grandfather hoped that he was not making the sound, because if he were then he must be in very bad shape. He just had time to remark that the sound was oddly familiar when an English bulldog even fatter and uglier yet moving far faster than Hadassah had ever moved in her life—maybe it was the example set by its thoroughbred neighbors—rolled in like an asthmatic bowling ball, paws slapping at the mud. In a single continuous motion it dropped what it had in its mouth, snatched the last sausage right off the fork, and rolled out again.

What it dropped from its teeth so that it could grab the sausage turned out to be a human ear, edged with blood. It landed on the grate with a soft plop and immediately began to sizzle. That was the last thing that my grandfather noticed for a little while.

When he came to he was lying on his side on a table in a room made of raw lumber and lath. There were jars of cotton and boxes of gauze and a heavy smell of camphor and pine tar. Lying on the floor beside the table where my grandfather lay was a male corpse, dressed in an elegant double-breasted suit. The side of its head was caked with black blood and it wore an expression of profound disappointment. It had lost an ear.

There was a chink of metal against metal. My grandfather rolled partway over and saw the stall man, wearing a white linen coat, at a workbench. There was a gas ring on the workbench with a pot of water boiling. The stall man was fishing stainless steel surgical implements out of the boiling water with a set of tongs and laying them out on a towel that lined a steel tray. He picked up the tray and turned to my grandfather.

"Did you kill him?"

"Nope. He just bled out."

"He was a German spy."

"Only appropriate, since he grew up in Germantown. Germantown High, he told me, Class of '26. Growl, You Bears."

"Are you Feuerman?"

"If that's what you heard."

"I have two questions."

"All right."

"Are there any more sausages?"

"Not impossible. Second question?"

"Am I going to bleed out, too?"

"Hope not."

"I don't want to die."

"Gotcha."

"Be straight with me. Can you fix me up?"

Feuerman set the tray down and pushed back the sleeves of his white coat, revealing the tattoos.

"'Let us try,'" he said.

FOR A LONG TIME—ALL HIS LIFE, PERHAPS LONGER—there were only hospital sounds, the rattle and squeak of a gurney's wheels, the cryptic bongs of the paging system, coughing. A lot of coughing. And then a man's voice, a soft Park Avenue drawl.

"Wake him up."

"I'm awake," my grandfather said. "Sir."

"You want to open your eyes, son?"

Gasping a little. Too many cigarettes, too many stairs taken too quickly. Somebody else on the other side of the bed, fidgeting with coins or keys.

"Last time I opened my eyes," my grandfather said, "I threw up."

"Might want to take a step back, Lovell."

Whisper of leather against linoleum.

"Okay, let her rip, son."

My grandfather opened his eyes. For the first second or two the world sloshed like a bucket but then it settled down. Bill Donovan and Stanley Lovell were keeping a respectful distance on either side of the bed he did not remember having been laid in, on a ward of a hospital he had been told, at some point, was Walter Reed. He had no idea how he had gotten to Walter Reed from Feuerman's trailer or how long it had been since the trainer had shot him up with a syringe full of something that could knock out a five-hundred-pound horse.

"Well?" Donovan said.

My grandfather said he thought they were probably safe to come a little closer. Lovell had gotten himself a haircut and had his mustache trimmed since their previous conversation which might be a good sign but on the other hand had made no adjustments in his air of annoyance with my grandfather. Donovan just stood there, in a double-breasted gray-on-navy pinstripe suit, beaming at my grandfather with what appeared to be unalloyed pride. He held out his big paw with its manicured nails and my grandfather shook it.

"Good Christ, son, did you ever make a mess of things," he said happily.

My grandfather looked at Lovell. He wanted to ask him about General Strong and the letter of resignation but while he struggled to figure out how to phrase the question discreetly it must have leaked out through his eyes.

"For the time being, yes," Lovell said, looking incrementally less irritated. "Thank you."

"I didn't do much."

"You got shot?" Donovan said.

"Yes, sir."

"And how was that?"

"It hurt like a bastard, sir."

"And then a crooked horse doctor stitched you up with some baling twine."

"It certainly feels that way."

"It was something of an ordeal, then. But in the end, you hunted your man down."

My grandfather supposed that this was, strictly speaking, the case.

"I guess you could say I located him."

"Is he going to bring any further dishonor to my dear friend and brother in arms General Strong, and his worthy band of bravos?"

"I doubt it, sir."

Donovan patted my grandfather on the shoulder.

"Let me ask you the most important question. Did you *enjoy* yourself?"

Surely, my grandfather thought, the answer to this question could not possibly be anything but *No*.

"Looking back," he said. "Yes, sir."

"Stanley says you've been itching to get out of the office a little."

"He wants to go *elsewhere*," Lovell said.

"And I'd like to send him elsewhere. Now that we've kicked open the door it's time to send some hunters in. Would it be fair, Lieutenant," Donovan said, turning on the courtroom manner, "and you'll pardon the technical jargon, but would it be fair to characterize you as a goddamn bloody-minded Philadelphia Jewboy gangster?"

My grandfather said he supposed the characterization, while not entirely accurate, would suffice.

"Would it also be fair to say you are a coolheaded clear-eyed man of science?"

"I'd like to think so."

Donovan smacked my grandfather on the knee and stood up.

"Well, good, because that's the kind of hunter we're going to need."

"Colonel, I have to tell you, by the time I got there, the guy was already—"

"Oh, for God's sake," Lovell said. "He doesn't care! You're getting what you wanted. Just shut the hell up and say thank you."

Despite his bloody-mindedness, my grandfather took Stanley Lovell's advice, though as a clear-eyed man of science he chose to proceed in a more logical fashion, first saying thank you to Donovan, and only then shutting the hell up.